Rita at
Rushybrook Farm

Rita at Rushybrook Farm

Hilda Offen

Happy Cat Books

For Bluebell

HAPPY CAT BOOKS

Published by Happy Cat Books Ltd.
Bradfield, Essex CO11 2UT, UK

First published 2003
3 5 7 9 10 8 6 4 2

A CIP catalogue record for this book is available from the British Library

ISBN 1 903285 42 9

Printed in China by Midas Printing Limited

"You'll like Rushybrook Farm!" said
Grandad Potter. "They've got pigs and cows
and horses."
"And there's face-painting!" said Julie.
"And buzzards!" said Jim. "There's going to
be a Flying Display."
Grandad Potter bought them each two bags
of birdseed.
"I'm going for a cup of tea," he said. "Look
after Rita."

5

"I'll take care of your birdseed, Rita," said
Eddie. "I don't suppose you'll need it."
"No – we've got just the place for you," said
Julie. "The Little Pets Barn. You can cuddle
kittens and rabbits."

They left her in the barn and ran away.
"Come and sit down," said the lady in
charge. "Here's a duckling for you to hold."
"Will you swap your duck for my wabbit?"
asked a little boy.
"Hmph!" said Rita to herself. "Cuddling
ducks? I don't think so. I'm off."

7

She dived behind a pile of straw. It only took
a moment to change into her Rescuer outfit.
No-one noticed as she shot out of the door.

The first thing Rita came across was the
Flying Display. Billy the Buzzard was
perching on people's heads.
"Keep perfectly still!" called the Bird Man.
"Billy is harmless!"

But Billy had seen something move.
Mrs. Gubbins had hidden her little
dog, Bobo, inside her coat.
  Billy pounced. He carried Bobo
away to the top of a fir tree.
"He's going to eat him!" shrieked
Mrs. Gubbins.
"Here, Billy!" called the Bird Man.
But Billy took no notice.
Rita came whirling through the air
and perched on Billy's branch.
"You won't like him!" she said. "He's
all bony and furry. He'll give you
hiccups."

"Hmm!" said Billy. He peered at Bobo.
"Perhaps you're right."
He pushed Bobo off the branch and flew
back to the Bird Man. Rita dived after Bobo
and caught him just before he hit the
ground.
"Oh, thank you, thank you, Rescuer!" cried
Mrs. Gubbins.

Meanwhile, Gypsy Joan was about to face-
paint Julie.
"What would you like?" she asked.
"Butterflies!" said Julie.

Eddie and Jim were exploring outside the caravan.

"What's this block of wood behind the back wheel?" wondered Eddie.

"I don't know!" said Jim. "There's one on my side, too."

Oh no! They shouldn't have touched them.

The caravan lumbered downhill. It went faster and faster.

"Help!" shrieked Gypsy Joan. "We're heading for the quarry!"

Rita heard the screams. She hurtled through the air and caught the caravan at the edge of a sheer drop. Then she pushed it back up the hill and replaced the wedges.

"Thank you, Rescuer!" cried Gypsy Joan. "Would you like your fortune told?"

"Yes, please!" said Rita.

"Ooh-er!" said Gypsy Joan. "I see another
rescue coming up! I see a small boy! I see a
pig!"
But she spoke to thin air. Rita was off!
Little Bertie Bates had climbed onto the
pigsty wall. He tripped on his shoelaces! He
fell backwards and landed on a pig's back.
The pig was so startled it leaped the wall
and galloped off into a wood.

"My prize pig!" cried Farmer Bell. "My Lady Pandora!"

"Never mind your prize pig!" snapped Mrs. Bates. "What about my Bertie?"

"We'll never find them!" cried Farmer Bell. "It's the deepest, darkest wood in the county."

Rita's nose twitched. "I'll find them for you," she said; and she raced off amongst the trees. Sniff! Sniff! She was hot on the trail.

At last she heard a wailing sound – and
there were Lady Pandora and Bertie, sinking
into a bog.
Rita didn't hesitate. She dived straight into
the mud and lifted them clear.

Then she cleaned them up with some moss
and they set off for home. Lady Pandora
carried them part of the way and then Rita
took over.

"My Bertie!" screamed Mrs. Bates as they
came into view.

"My Lady Pandora!" cried Farmer Bell.

"I've got to go!" said Rita. "I see trouble."

There was uproar by the duckpond. It was Eddie! He was being attacked by a flock of fowls. They were after the birdseed in his rucksack.

"Ow! Get off!" yelled Eddie as a turkey lunged at him; and the next moment he lost his balance and toppled into the water.

The seed was so heavy that Eddie sank straight to the bottom.
Splash! Rita dived in after him and pulled him to the bank. Then she huffed him dry with her hot breath.

19

What was that rumbling noise?
Oh no! A stack of strawbales had collapsed!

They thundered down the hill towards the paddock where the children were feeding the lambs.

"Biff ! Pow ! Wallop!"
Rita kicked the bales back
up the hill.

"Hooray!" cried the children. "Well saved!
You could play in goal for England,
Rescuer!"
"Do you think so?" said Rita. "Uh-oh! I'm
off again."
She could hear a lot of screaming
and neighing.

Daisy the carthorse had been stung by a bee! She was out of control. She galloped along with four children clinging to her back.

"Whoa, Daisy!" cried Rita and she somersaulted through the air and grabbed Daisy's reins.

They skidded to a halt at the edge of the Tea Garden.

"You're a star, Rescuer!" said Farmer Bell.
"Have a milk shake – have two! Have three!
Have as much ice-cream as you like!"
"Thank you, Farmer Bell!" said Rita. She
finished everything up. "Mm! Lovely!" she
said.

Then she flew back to the Little Pets
Barn and changed out of her outfit.
"There you are, Rita!" said Eddie.
"Come on - we'll miss the bus."

"You should have seen the Rescuer!" said
Julie on the way home. "She saved me from
the quarry."
"She saved me from a crowd of mad birds!"
said Eddie.
"And she saved me from being trampled by
a carthorse!" said Grandad Potter.
"How did you get on with the Little Pets,
Rita?" asked Jim. "Did you have a good
day?"
"Yes, I did!" said Rita. "It was marvellous."

Other Rita titles available in Happy Cat Paperbacks

Arise, Our Rita!

Rita may be the youngest of the Potter family, but she also is the fabulous Rescuer! And teaching archery to Robin Hood, taming dragons and giants, is all in a day's work for our pint-sized superhero.

Happy Christmas, Rita!

On a snowy day Rita is stuck inside with no coat to wear – but she does have her Rescuer's outfit! And on the day before Christmas she has some daring and important rescues to perform, including rescuing Father Christmas himself!

Rita the Rescuer

When you are the youngest in the family, you can sometimes get left out of the fun. Then one day Rita Potter is sent a magical Rescuer's outfit which gives her amazing powers… Three cheers for Rita!

Rita and the Romans

Left behind in the Potter family's Wendy-house it is lucky Rita has her Rescuer's outfit to hand. In no time at all she is rescuing toddlers, saving gladiators and even building Adrian's Wall!